YOU'RE NOT MY BEST FRIEND ANYMORE

by Charlotte Pomerantz
pictures by
David Soman

DIAL BOOKS FOR YOUNG READERS
NEW YORK

For Jane Clement Bond
C.P.

For Amy
D.S.

Published by Dial Books for Young Readers
A Division of Penguin Books USA Inc.
375 Hudson Street
New York, New York 10014

Designed by Julie Rauer
Printed in Hong Kong
First Edition
1 3 5 7 9 10 8 6 4 2

Library of Congress Cataloging in Publication Data
Pomerantz, Charlotte.
You're not my best friend anymore/by Charlotte Pomerantz;
pictures by David Soman.
p. cm.
Summary: Molly and Ben are best friends and
share everything until they have a fight.
ISBN 0-8037-1559-5.—ISBN 0-8037-1560-9 (lib. bdg.)
[1. Friendship—Fiction.] I. Soman, David, ill. II. Title.
PZ7.P77Yo 1998 [E]—dc20 93-42595 CIP AC

The art was rendered in watercolor on plate-finished paper.

MOLLY AND BEN were best friends.

They lived in a two-family house. Molly lived with her father and
mother on the ground floor.

   Ben lived with his father and his aunt one flight up. They all shared
a front stoop and a backyard.

Molly and Ben walked to school together.

They ate at the same
table in the lunchroom.

After school they played

and did their homework together.
Sometimes they wore the same T-shirts.

They even celebrated their birthdays together. Ben was born on
June 5. Molly was born on June 15. So they had a double birthday
party on June 10.

Molly's parents liked the idea. Ben's father said it was easier to bake
two cakes at one time. Ben's aunt said she liked big parties.

On Saturdays Molly and Ben often went downtown to spend their allowances. They didn't go every Saturday. Sometimes they would save for weeks and weeks and buy one big thing that they both wanted. Right now they were saving for a tent.

One day, a week before the double birthday party, Molly and Ben had a fight. Not a little fight—about which program to watch on TV. Or who should put the books and toys away. Or whose front teeth stuck out the most.

It was a big fight. It was about the kind of tent they should buy with all the allowance they had saved. Molly wanted a pup tent. Ben wanted an umbrella tent.

"You can't stand up in a pup tent," said Ben.

"Who wants to stand up?" said Molly. "A tent is for sleeping."

"Well, I like to stand up," said Ben.

"An umbrella tent is dumb," said Molly.

"A pup tent is dumb," said Ben.

"You're dumb," said Molly. "I'm going home."

"Good," said Ben. "Don't call me up unless it's an emergency."

"Emergency," snorted Molly. "What sort of emergency would make me call you?"

Ben shrugged. "I don't know," he said. "Maybe if the house caught on fire."

"That's the dumbest thing I ever heard," said Molly. "We live in the same house."

"So don't call!" screamed Ben. "Even if the house is on fire." He slammed the door.

Molly opened it. "By the way," she shouted, "you're not my best friend anymore!"

The rest of the week
they walked to school
on different sides
of the street.

They sat
at different
tables
in the
lunchroom.

They didn't wear the same T-shirts and they didn't do
their homework or play together after school.

Molly wrote in her diary:

Dear Diary,
I told my mom that I wanted
to go camping by myself.
My mom said no way.
I hate Ben. I wish he
would move to Juneau,
which is the capital of Alaska.

Ben wrote in his diary:

*My dad says that I can camp
out in the backyard with
a friend. Who needs friends?
I hate Molly. I wish I had
a puppy.*

Molly and Ben didn't speak to each other for four days. Then Ben saw Molly sitting on the front stoop. He shifted from one foot to another. "By the way," he said, "my father wants to know when you are having your birthday party."

Molly looked suspicious. "Your father?" she said. "How come your father wants to know?"

"Because," said Ben, "he bakes the cakes, remember?"

Molly sighed. "I guess we should have one party for the sake of the grown-ups. After all, they buy all the birthday stuff."